Conrad, Pam.
Don't go near that rabbit,
Frank!

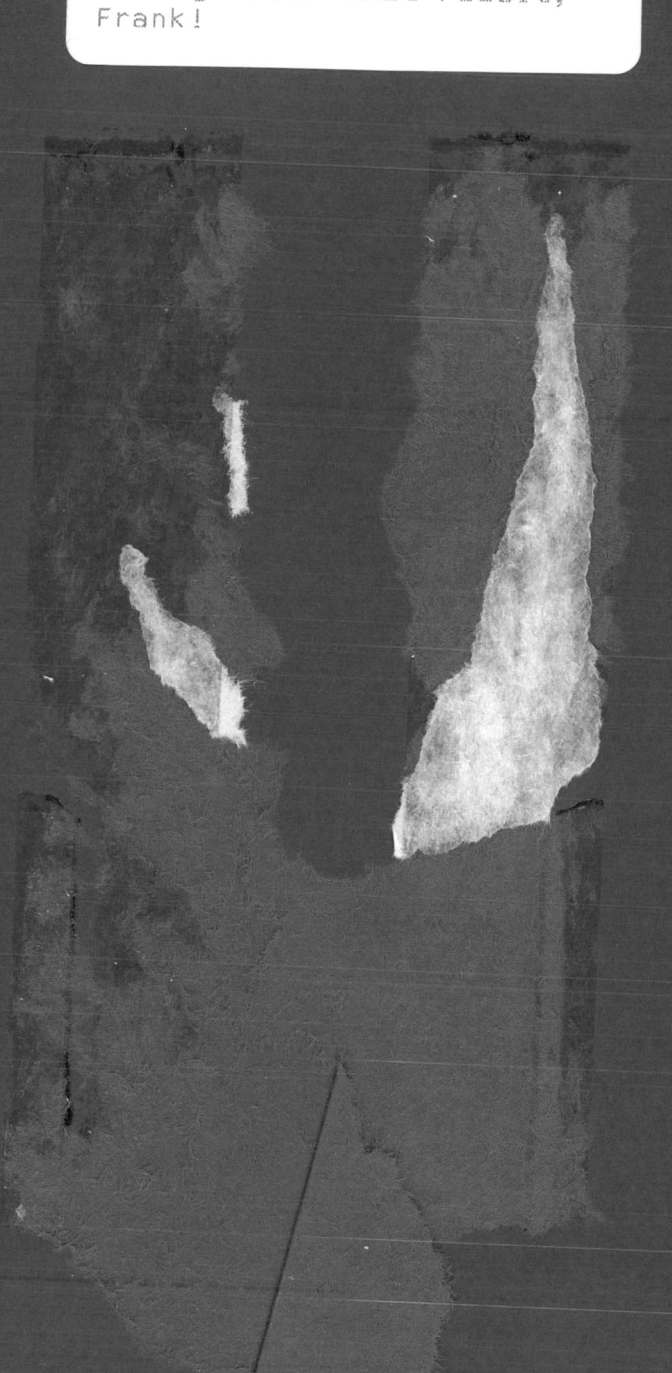

DON'T GO NEAR THAT RABBIT, FRANK!

. . .

by PAM CONRAD

illustrated by
MARK ENGLISH

A LAURA GERINGER BOOK
An Imprint of HarperCollinsPublishers

Don't Go Near That Rabbit, Frank!
Text copyright © 1998 by the Estate of Pamela Conrad
Illustrations copyright © 1998 by Mark English
Printed in the U.S.A. All rights reserved.

Library of Congress Cataloging-in-Publication Data
Conrad, Pam.
    Don't go near that rabbit, Frank! / by Pam Conrad ; illustrated by Mark English.
    "A Laura Geringer book."
        p.   cm.
    Summary: When their playful dog comes home with a dead rabbit, Philip and Kooch are
afraid it is their gruff old neighbor's prize pet.
    ISBN 0-06-021514-3
    [1. Dogs—Fiction.   2. Brothers and sisters—Fiction.]   I. English, Mark, ill.   II. Title.
PZ7.C76476Do   1998   94-45773
[Fic]—dc20   CIP
                                                                                            AC

Designed by Christine Kettner
1   2   3   4   5   6   7   8   9   10
❖
First Edition
Visit the HarperCollins Children's Books web site at
http://www.harperchildrens.com

PHILIP RUSSELL JENKINS and his sister, Kooch, lived at the edge of a brand-new neighborhood that had been built right where Old Man Hoover's potato farm used to be. Not many people knew it had been a farm. But the Jenkins family knew, because they lived on the edge of the neighborhood, and their neighbor on the west fence was Old Man Hoover himself and his wife, Mrs. Hoover.

The Hoovers lived in the same old house they had lived in for over fifty years. Only now instead of looking out over acres and acres of potatoes, they looked out at Philip's house, and at all the other houses with their symmetrical roofs and chimneys and neatly clipped lawns.

When Philip and his sister were younger and had first moved to the neighborhood, their father bought them a puppy that their mother named Frank. Frank was more like a bear cub than a puppy, with his big feet and his wide mouth. And everyone was sure he'd grow into a handsome pet.

Everyone, that is, except Old Man Hoover.

OLD MAN HOOVER stood glaring at Frank across the fence. The giant trees behind him made him seem almost like a dwarf in the snow. "If that dog comes anywhere near my prize rabbit," he warned them, "I'll load my rifle and shoot him dead."

Frank, the puppy, not understanding a word the old man said, romped through the snow to where Old Man Hoover stood and threw himself against the fence in a fit of abandoned joy.

"What prize rabbit is that, Mr. Hoover?" asked Philip's mother, ignoring the part that Philip wanted to ask, which was: *What rifle is that?*

"Come around to the front gate," Old Man Hoover demanded. "I'll show you." But he sounded like they were interrupting something important.

"A rabbit!" said Kooch. "A real rabbit with fur and rabbit's feet! Can we go see him, Ma? Can we? Can we?" Kooch jumped up and down, and Philip thought she might throw herself against the fence just like Frank had.

Mrs. Jenkins scooped up Frank from the snow and shooed him in the back door to their kitchen. "Yes, let's go see the rabbit. And maybe we can get to know this cantankerous old farmer."

The Jenkinses had been living in their new house since the autumn, and Old Man Hoover had barely nodded to them before. Now he was opening the front gate, and when he saw them coming, he turned without a word and walked toward his barn. They followed him to a small wooden hutch that was nestled on the ground. There was a well-worn path all around it in the snow, icicles as thick as Philip's thumbs hanging from the sides, and inside was the fattest, most gigantic rabbit Philip and Kooch had ever seen.

It slept against the chicken wire, and a fringe of white fur stuck out. Kooch smoothed her fingers through it and sighed. Philip didn't know what the old man was worried about. He could see there was no way Frank could get at that rabbit. No way.

Old Man Hoover lifted the latch on the hutch and coaxed the fat rabbit out into his arms. A smile crept across his face and looked as awkward there as fine china on a barbecue table.

"Old Peter here is fifteen years old. Won ten blue ribbons himself in best of breed and has sired count-less offspring that have gone on to win awards too." He held the fat rabbit in his arms like you'd hold a fat pig. Philip hadn't known rabbits could get so big.

Kooch touched the fur with both hands.

"Mommy, look at his pink nose and his pink eyes."
Peter's back leg twitched lazily.

"Yessir, there was a time when rabbit raising
was serious business around here, before those
cracker boxes—" He motioned with his chin to
Philip's house and the neighborhood that spread
out beyond it.

"Oscar! How nice. Why didn't you tell me we
had company?"

Coming across the yard, clear plastic boots on
her feet and a green shawl wrapped around her
shoulders, was Mrs. Hoover. If Peter was the
largest rabbit Philip had ever seen, Mrs. Hoover
was the smallest old lady he'd ever seen. She was
not much bigger than Kooch, and her hands and
feet were smaller, but Philip could tell that unlike
Frank and his sister, Mrs. Hoover wasn't going to
get any bigger.

Philip's mother extended her hand to Mrs.

Hoover, who took it in both her own. "Nice to meet you, Mrs. Hoover. I'm Katie Jenkins from next door, and these are my children, Philip Russell and Kooch."

"Oh, and I just made some delicious chocolate-chip cookies. How did I know we'd be having company? Well, come along." Mrs. Hoover clapped her tiny hands and headed back to the house without waiting to hear what Old Man Hoover had to say. "Oscar," she commanded over her shoulder, "bring Peter into the house awhile, and we'll show our neighbors all his awards."

The Hoovers' house was as tiny as they were. Small hooked rugs were scattered here and there. The chairs were all small, with tiny lace doilies pinned to their arms. Philip's mother's head almost touched the ceiling beams. Once they were inside, they all removed their boots. Mrs. Hoover secured the door. Then Old Man Hoover let Peter down on the floor, and the rabbit ran right for the fireplace, where he scrambled in over the pile of wood and settled down.

"Come out of there, Peter!" the old man scolded. "You see, Gloria, he doesn't listen in here. I never should have brought him in. Now look. He's full of soot."

Mrs. Hoover winked at the children. "The old man thinks that rabbit is a genius, and fact is, he's as dumb as a stump. Old Peter, that is. Some tea, Mrs. Jenkins?"

Philip watched the old man lift the rabbit from the fireplace and brush him off carefully. The entire fat underside of the rabbit was black. "Now look. Now look," Old Man Hoover was muttering. "I just wanted to warn these youngsters to keep their hound dog away from our hutch, that's all. Had no intentions of inviting the entire family for dinner."

"Hush. Hush," the old woman scolded, and

just as Philip's mother had shooed Frank into the kitchen, the old woman shooed her husband and the giant rabbit out the door.

When she brought the cookies in, she whispered, "I don't know what Oscar would do if anything ever happened to that rabbit. It's all he has left of our farm, you know. I don't know what he'd do."

Old Mrs. Hoover shook her head wistfully, and while she showed Kooch and her mother the album of all Peter's awards and newspaper clippings, Philip stared at Old Man Hoover's rifle, which stood behind the door. He thought of Frank and what the old man had said.

If that dog comes anywhere near my prize rabbit, I'll load my rifle and shoot him dead. That's exactly what he had said.

Philip thought of his frisky new puppy, and the cookies in his mouth turned to sand.

FRANK, THE PUPPY, grew as his large padded feet had promised. He grew faster than the children and soon weighed more than either of them. But Philip's father said that size was no indication of intelligence, and that Frank, now considered to be a man of sorts, in dog years, couldn't find a flea on a glass table.

This was true. Frank's favorite activity was to snore blissfully in Kooch's arms before the television set. Philip was terribly disappointed that Frank wasn't more of a rascal, and that he wouldn't tear through the neighborhood alongside him on the bike, but at least Philip didn't have to worry about Frank going near Old Man Hoover's rabbit.

That was a laugh. Philip's mother said that Frank was so far down the ancestral scale from his original forebears that he didn't have any instincts left. He loved the mailman, slept through the doorbell, and Philip was sure that even if Frank had come across a rabbit through some quirk, he never would have known what to do with it. Philip was pretty sure of this.

You can never be too sure.

One awful summer evening, after dinner, Philip and Kooch were out playing. Philip was riding his bike and Kooch was on skates, holding on to the seat and getting a pull up and down the straight blocks, around the round blocks, and up and back the dead ends. Here and there sprinklers were dappling the hot cement and their legs with mist, and school friends called out to them.

It seemed like a perfect summer day. Philip and Kooch hardly noticed how the sky was growing darker and darker. Then clusters of boys on bikes scattered away like black summer wasps, and women began pulling dry clothes off their wash lines. Soon the entire sky was black and all the world seemed like a dark room. But still Philip and Kooch raced on. Their parents had gone to a movie, and the two of them were on their own. No one called and said, *Come on in, it's going to rain.* No one said, *What, are you crazy? Get in here!* So they biked and skated until a drop as big as a frog hit Kooch right in her face. Then Philip got one on his hand, then his handlebars, and then the whole world turned to water. They screamed and laughed and raced back to their house as fast as they could.

Philip ran his bike into the garage, and they

dove for the house. They were both as wet as if they'd been dumped in a carnival dunking barrel, and because no one was home they laughed and pointed at each other.

Unfortunately, the laughing woke Frank.

He yawned and stretched and slowly pulled himself from the sofa. He sat down between Philip and Kooch and sniffed the air absentmindedly. He stared at the puddles at their feet. And while Kooch peeled off her wet socks, he scratched lazily at the door.

"What, are you crazy?" Philip asked. "It's pouring out there."

Frank scratched again and cried a little.

"Frank! Not now! We're not taking you out until it stops raining," Kooch told him.

But Frank scratched again.

"All right," said Philip. "Look!" And at that he threw open the door, and Frank backed away in

horror. "I told you," Philip said, closing the door on the torrential rain.

But as soon as the door closed, Frank was scratching and sniffing at it again.

"He's gotta go," Kooch said.

"So you take him out," Philip said.

"He'll wet in the house," Kooch warned.

Philip and Kooch stared at Frank, who was by now leaning his head back and moaning deep in his throat.

"Frank!" Kooch shouted.

"Let's just send him out alone," Philip said. "He won't go far. He hates the rain."

"Ma says not to do that. You should walk him."

They sat there on the steps. Frank sat at the door and howled.

"Oh, all right," said Kooch. She got up and opened the door and told Frank to go ahead. But he sat there, sniffing the air, staring in lazy dismay at the storm. Kooch nudged him, but he dug in. "Come on, Philip, help me." Then the two of them, with all their might, got behind Frank and pushed him out the door into the rain. The minute he was out, they locked the door and grinned at each other.

"Think he'll make it to the bushes?" Philip asked.

"He probably won't even leave the front door," Kooch guessed.

Then Philip and Kooch went into the kitchen to find a cloth to dry the puddles. They didn't even think about Frank again till much later. And neither of them thought about Old Man Hoover's rabbit at all. That is, not until they heard the scratch at the door and opened it wide. "Frank!" Philip cried. "I'm sorry! We forgot all about—"

And there stood big old Frank in the doorway,

wet and dripping, his paws full of mud, his tail swishing like a tiller in the rain, and hanging from his mouth, unbelievable as this may seem, was a huge dead rabbit. A white one.

"Oh, no, Frank—what have you done?" Philip whispered.

Kooch came to the front door just as Frank dropped the tremendous rabbit before them on the floor and smiled. "Oh!" Kooch's hands flew to her mouth. "Oh, Frank!"

Both of them were on their knees before the big dog. "You killed Old Man Hoover's rabbit, Frank! I don't believe it. I don't believe it."

Kooch thought Philip was going to cry. "I'd better call Mrs. Hoover," she said, turning for the kitchen.

"No! Don't do that!" her brother shouted. "Don't you remember? Old Man Hoover will shoot Frank. That's what he said when we first moved in

here. 'If that dog comes anywhere near my prize rabbit,' he said, 'I'll load my rifle and shoot him dead.'"

"What are we gonna do, Philip? What are we gonna do? Oh, Frank, I can't believe you killed a rabbit. Old Man Hoover's rabbit."

They stared as Frank shook himself halfheartedly and wandered away into the living room. The dead rabbit lay limp in a puddle in the middle of their front hall.

Philip reached out and placed his hand on its muddy fur. He waited. "No heartbeat." He lifted its leg. Limp. Nothing. Its pink nose was dipped in mud.

"Oh, I wish Mom and Dad were here," Kooch whined. "They'd know what to do."

"It's a good thing Mom and Dad *aren't* here," Philip said almost to himself. "We've got to get this rabbit back in its hutch. Come on. Help me."

Together Philip and Kooch lifted the dead muddy rabbit in their arms, slippery and stiff between them, and to Kooch's horror Philip led the way up the stairs and to the bathroom.

"Philip! What are you doing?"

He placed the dead rabbit in the middle of the bathtub, pushed down the plug, and turned on the water full blast. He rolled up his sleeves and glared at Kooch. "Don't tell a soul, Kooch, you hear? You never saw this rabbit. He was never here. And Frank didn't do it."

"But Philip, what are you going to do?"

"We're going to make this rabbit look like nothing happened."

"But he's dead!"

"Gimme the shampoo," he said.

When the rabbit was all clean and smelling

faintly of rosewater, Philip wrapped him in one of his father's big bath towels and laid him on his parents' bed. The rabbit was dripping wet, its fur flat like the scales on a fish. Kooch stood in the doorway, staring while Philip started to rub the fur briskly.

"This is going to take forever," he complained. Outside, the rain was easing up, and it was dark from the night now. His parents would be home soon.

"How about Mom's hair dryer?" Kooch asked quietly.

Philip's face lit up. "Yes! Go get it!"

And while Kooch held the rabbit up, Philip blow-dried its belly, and then while he held it, Kooch dried its back and under its ears. They were just about done, the rabbit as fluffy and clean as the day they had first met it, when they heard the front door open downstairs.

"Quick!"

"Hurry!"

"Wha—!"

"Go! Go!"

"Philip! Kooch!" The last was their mother's voice.

And then—"Oh, no! What did that dog do? Look at this mess! Where are you? Come down here this instant!"

Philip and Kooch panicked, scooped up the rabbit, ran to Philip's room, and slid the rabbit under his bed. "What are we gonna do? Does she know? Does she know?"

"Just pretend nothing happened," Philip warned her. "Just act like nothing in the world happened."

Together they went down the stairs and into the living room. Frank trailed behind them.

They found their mother pulling the cushions

off the sofa. They were caked with mud and rain. "Philip, you know better than this. How can you take Frank for a walk and then not dry him off? Please, Philip! Go get a towel. Get the vacuum cleaner. Look at this mess."

"Yes, Mom, I'm sorry." Philip nudged Kooch as he went to the closet for the vacuum.

"I'll get the towel," Kooch said, and as she passed, Philip reminded her in a whisper, "And remember, nothing happened. Nothing happened at all."

HILIP LAY AWAKE STARING at the ceiling. Waiting. Waiting. He listened to the sounds in the house. His father went into the bathroom. He could hear him brushing his teeth and humming. Then his mother went into the bathroom and Philip heard them talking and laughing.

Then there were the sounds of drawers opening and closing, bedsprings sighing, a window opening wider in the hot summer night, and then at last it grew very, very quiet.

And Philip kept waiting. The clock in the downstairs hall bonged twelve soft times. He could hear

Frank snoring in his sister's room. It wasn't
till an hour later, when the clock bonged just once,
that Philip slid carefully out of bed and pulled his
high-tops over his bare feet. He slipped into
his shorts and silently, silently dragged the soft
parcel out from under his bed. It was the dead
rabbit wrapped in his father's big bath towel. He
held it in both arms and stood motionless in
the doorway to his room, listening for sounds in
the hall. Nothing. Everyone was asleep. Cautiously
he made his way across the hall to the top of
the steps. As his foot creaked softly on the first
step—

"Philip."

"Shhhhhhhh!" he nearly shouted. Kooch's
head peeked around her doorway.

"Where are you going? What are you going to
do?"

"Shhh," he repeated, this time quietly, as he

shook his head and motioned her to follow him. Once they were at the back door, he turned to her. "I'm going to put old Peter here back in his hutch."

"Why?"

"So he's where he belongs."

"But Philip, he's still dead."

"I know that. And pretty soon Old Man Hoover's gonna know that. But he's not going to know Frank did it. If he knew, he'd shoot him."

"But what if he sees you? What if he catches you? He'll shoot you, too!"

Philip stared through the screen door out into the summer darkness. "Kind of like that story Mom used to read us about Peter Rabbit not being allowed to go into Mr. McGregor's garden."

Kooch's smile flashed in the darkness. "You gonna hide in a watering can?"

"Not unless I have to," he answered.

"Can't I go with you?" she pleaded.

"No. You wait here. If you hear any shooting, get Dad."

"Aw—"

But Philip was out the back door before she could say another word. The ground was still wet from the storm, and the maples overhead dripped tree-rain with every soft breeze. Somewhere nearby, a frog was singing in a puddle, and the stars were slowly appearing. Philip crept across his yard to the west fence. In the moonlight he lowered the clean, towel-wrapped rabbit over the edge of the fence and then hopped over the fence himself. He gathered the rabbit up in his arms once again and tiptoed across Old Man Hoover's yard to the hutch. His moon shadow led the way.

The old wooden hutch hunkered in the sweet grass in the shadow of the ancient oak tree. Philip was careful to step over a metal pail beside it. Somewhere in the neighborhood there was a loud sneeze, and then it grew quiet again.

Philip laid the dead rabbit gently on the ground and unwrapped the thick towel for a moment. The rabbit glowed white and clean in the night. "Okay, Peter," Philip said quietly, lifting the latch on the hutch. "You get back here where you belong and die a peaceful, natural death, so Old Man Hoover can find you exactly like this."

He lifted the gigantic dead rabbit and pushed it into the hutch off to one side, so its white fur made a little fringe through the metal squares of the chicken wire. Suddenly a small hand reached out and stroked it.

"Cripes!" yelled Philip. Then he whispered, "I thought I told you to stay home." Just like the rabbit, Kooch's white gown glowed in the moonlight.

"I just wanted to say good-bye one last time,"

she said, and dreamily smoothed the rabbit's fur. "He was so beautiful, Philip, wasn't he?"

"Would you please get out of here. You're shining like a light bulb in those pajamas."

Kooch looked down at herself and then up at the moon, which was wearing a frail rainbow if you didn't look too close. "Nobody here to see," she said.

Then suddenly, a few blocks away, over the croaking of the frogs, the volunteer firemen's siren began to wail, louder than seemed necessary; and startled, with cries of terror locked in their throats, Philip Russell and his sister, Kooch, flew wildly to the fence, dove over it into the rain-soaked grass, and, hardly breathing, tore into the house and up into their rooms. In the darkness, Philip felt his rain-soaked high-tops tangle in the sheets and his heart pound in his chest.

In the next room, he could hear Kooch creeping into her bed, telling Frank to *move over, move over, you big galoot.* Philip smiled with relief. He was sure Frank was safe now.

OR THE NEXT COUPLE of days, every time Philip went out the back door, he would look over into the Hoovers' yard, but it was hard to see the hutch. He couldn't tell if the dead rabbit was still there. Surely Old Man Hoover had found it by now. Surely the danger was over.

That weekend there was a craft fair in the meadow beyond Old Man Hoover's house. Tents and tables and awnings were set up, and beneath them neighbors were selling quilted pillows, carved wooden toys, and little people made out of nails and bolts. The Jenkins family had taken a walk to the fair with Frank at their sides. The August sun was beating down hard.

"Ma! Dad! Look! There's the old Hoovers selling something." Kooch pointed to a table and the Hoovers.

Old Man Hoover was standing there sulking with his hands in his overall pockets, and Mrs. Hoover was sitting in a folding chair shielded from the sun by an umbrella rigged to the chair.

"Kooch! No!" Philip muttered under his breath, pulling Frank's leash tight. But it was too late.

"Oh," said his mother. "Let's see what they're selling." And she headed right for their table.

"You'd better watch it, Philip," Kooch said, stepping alongside him. "You-know-what is written all over your face."

"How dumb can you get?" Philip said. "I mean why don't you just invite Old Man Hoover to take a look in Frank's mouth for rabbit hairs?"

"Oh, stop it. All the rabbit hairs are gone by now."

Mrs. Hoover looked up at the Jenkinses as they approached, and she smiled. "Why, hello, neighbors," she said cheerily. Before her on the table were little doilies in all colors to hang in windows, to put under bottles of perfume, or to pin to the arms of tiny chairs. But no sooner had they approached the table than Old Man Hoover hung his head, turned on his heel, and walked quickly away.

Uh-oh, thought Philip. *He's gone to get his rifle*. He pulled Frank to his side protectively and patted his barrel chest.

"Oh, don't mind him," Mrs. Hoover said. "He's in a bad way this week, I'm afraid." She looked at Philip and Kooch's mother, and bending close over her crocheted doilies, she whispered hoarsely, "Lost his rabbit."

"Oh, I'm so sorry," their mother said.

"Well, it was bound to happen sooner or later," the old woman said, "but it's just the way that it happened that was so peculiar."

Philip looked over his shoulder to see if the old man was coming back with his rifle, but he'd gotten lost in the clusters of people.

"Do you remember that bad rainstorm we had a couple of nights ago?" Mrs. Hoover continued. "Came down like crazy, drops as big as biscuits?"

"We were at the movies," Philip's mother answered. "I missed that one, but the kids were home, and the dog. He sure made a mess that night."

Philip almost clamped his hand over his mother's mouth, but Mrs. Hoover didn't seem to take much notice.

"You see, right before that rain started, Oscar went out to the rabbit hutch to make sure old Peter was in tight before the storm, and the poor old thing was dead as a post. Old Peter, that is."

Philip and Kooch stared at each other.

"So before the rain started, crying like a baby all the while, Oscar dug a hole and buried his old friend. I saw him with my own eyes, or I might have just chalked the whole thing up to Oscar's forgetfulness." She shook her head sadly.

"What do you mean?" their mother asked. Neither Philip nor Kooch was breathing.

"Well, the rabbit wouldn't stay buried."

"What?"

Philip was all ears.

"Well, after Oscar buried old Peter—and believe me, I saw him with my own eyes right out the kitchen window—he came in and went right to bed. Nothing would bring him down. Not even *The Honeymooners* on TV. Not even a rainbow around the moon. It was as if his heart was broken."

They were waiting for the rest.

"But the next morning Oscar went out to tear down the hutch, and don't you know old Peter was back in it, clean and dry like he was still living and wouldn't stay dead. He was still dead all right, so Oscar had to bury him all over again. But we don't know what to make of it. The most peculiar thing. And of course Oscar won't take down the hutch now, in case Peter comes back, you know."

Philip and Kooch were grinning at each other, and before they could stop themselves, they began to giggle.

"Philip! Kooch! Stop that!" Their mother was staring at them in shock, but they couldn't stop. It bubbled up inside them, even with Mrs. Hoover standing there with her mouth open. Without another word the two of them—with Frank at their heels—took off away from the little table, the craft fair, and the little meadow and headed back toward home.

Once there, they threw themselves on their front lawn where the potatoes used to grow, and they rolled around hugging Frank. Their laughter spread up the block like smoke from a summer barbecue, and when neighbors looked out their windows to see what was going on, they could see Philip Russell Jenkins and his sister, Kooch, sprawled on the lawn with their dog, Frank. And Frank, true to himself, was lying on his back with all four paws aimed up into the maple trees, where the summer locusts rattled on and on and on.